P9-DVB-797

The Names of the Rapids

The Names of the Rapids

JONATHAN HOLDEN

The University of Massachusetts Press

Amherst, 1985

Printed in the United States of America
Set in Linoterm Weiss at The University of Massachusetts Press
Printed and bound by Cushing-Malloy, Inc.

Library of Congress Cataloging-in-Publication Data
Holden, Jonathan.
The names of the rapids.
I. Title.
PS3558.034775N3 1985 811'.54 85-8751
ISBN 0-87023-501-X (alk. paper)
ISBN 0-87023-502-8 (pbk.: alk. paper)

For my father, Alan Nordby Holden

Contents

1. *The Names of the Rapids*

2. *Ramanujan*

Acknowledgments

The author and publisher wish to thank the following magazines for permission to reprint certain poems:

Aspen Anthology, for "Tornado Symptoms"; *Black Warrior Review*, for "Car Showroom"; *Cimarron Review*, for "The Kite"; *Colorado North Review*, for "Kansas Fair"; *Crosscurrents*, for "The Mercator Projection" and "The Scientist"; *Dacotah Territory*, for "Saturday Morning"; *Denver Quarterly*, for "'Early Sunday Morning,' by Edward Hopper" and "What to Do with Time on Your Hands"; *Georgia Review*, for "The Names of the Rapids"; *Indiana Review*, for "Night: Driving the Blizzard"; *Iowa Review*, for "River Time" and "Tinkering"; *Kansas Quarterly*, for "Water Poem"; *Kenyon Review*, for "The History of the Wedge" and "An Introduction to New Jersey"; *Mid-American Review*, for "Recessional"; *Minnesota Review*, for "Buying a Baseball" and "'The Swing,' by Honoré Fragonard"; *Missouri Review*, for "Facing West"; *Nimrod*, for "The Cattails"; *Ohio Review*, for "I Lie Awake on Top of the Sheets"; *Paris Review*, for "Roller Coaster"; *Plainsong*, for "Fireworks"; *Poetry*, for "Full Moon, Rising," "Rereading Old Love Letters," "Scraping the House," and "Wading"; *Poetry Now*, for "Lines Written from Central Kansas"; *Prairie Schooner*, for "Ramanujan"; *Quarry West*, for "'Snap the Whip,' by Winslow Homer"; *Quarterly West*, for "Casino" and "On a Mild October Evening"; *Sou'wester*, for "Cutting Loose on an August Night"; *Three Rivers Poetry Journal*, for "Jim."

1

The Names of the Rapids

The Names of the Rapids

Snaggle-Tooth, Maytag, Taylor Falls—
long before we measured with our eyes
the true size of each monstrosity
its name, downriver, was famous to us.
It lay in wait, something to be slain
while our raft, errant, eddied
among glancing pinpricks of sun
and every bend giving way to bend
seemed a last reprieve.
But common terror has a raw taste.
It's all banality, as when
you stare straight into a bad cut—
this sense of being slightly more
awake than you might like.
When the raft pitches sideways off
a ledge, what you land on is less
than its name. It's a mechanism. None
of the demented expressions
that the fleshly water forms
over that stone profile
is more than another collision,
a fleeting logic lost and
forming, now lost in the melee.
When the world is most serious
we approach it with wholly open eyes
even as we start the plunge
and the stone explanation.

Wading

Around each glittering loop
of that chill treble brook
above Lake Isabelle,
gingerly, we'd balance
from one rock to the next,
staggering when their blades
dented the tender cups
of our bare feet, but
welcoming that pain.
I think we needed it
to help us feel the world
enough, to be complete.
Back then, the snow-melt's hurt
was luxury, like salt,
before our children came—
we fell all the way in—
and the world put us to work.
We'd follow each haphazard
instruction of the brook,
lingering on the shelves
where it relaxed, shilly-shallying
in laps of red-gold gravel,
dangling our feet
until we'd lost all track
of where our feet had been
though we could see them in there,
swollen and white, still clear,
silly among the stones.
We gazed in. The clock
of the water was so pure
you couldn't have told it was there
except in the interior
the stones throbbing together

all deepened color, it was always
a slightly later time
of day. We gazed down in
as if for something missing,
gazed into the world
where we were wading.

The Cattails

The waist-deep water was sick gray, filmed
with oily rainbows. There was no
ground. The bottom was that soft—like clouds—
and treacherous. We couldn't see. Each time
you felt one footstep forward to a cloud
the cloud rolled up your leg and drew it
down. The leg was being enveloped by wet
hands. Your heart constricted. Your leg
was gradually disappearing under you. As you
succumbed, the voices of The Great Swamp swarmed
around your hair. It didn't care, it just went
on, the menacing hum of everything tensely
minding its own business. Your other boot
tore up with a gagging sound, broke water
with a thrash. So we forced our way forward
again toward the cattails standing like sticks
of dynamite on the ends of their stiff fuses.

Dried out, teased with matches, they fumed
for hours, the punks we used to light our
firecrackers with. I see some now, salvos
of skyrockets taking off gracefully on their
stems, but it's mid-December, and to get out there
and wrench the stems apart I'd have to pad across
black ice that twinges when you nick it
with a stone. It wouldn't support me anymore,
and there are signs here now. It is unlawful
to leave the boardwalk or disturb this swamp.
It is a National Preserve. Looking down now
at the ice, I can see it all—the rotten logs
locked in like corpses in glass cases, tufts
of grasses freeze-dried into tufts of brittle fire,
the rich clouds we foundered in, through which

I writhed, a smooth stratus that would barely wet
my knees—all collected, all changed
to a museum; and I just don't know anymore
if I wouldn't rather see the whole swamp torn
up and covered with mailboxes, streetlights, anything,
than all those beautiful cattails stuck out there.

Car Showroom

Day after day, along with his placid
automobiles, that well-groomed
sallow young man had been waiting for
me, as in the cheerful, unchanging
weather of a billboard—pacing
the tiles, patting his tie, knotting, un-
knotting the facade of his smile
while staring out the window.
He was so bad at the job
he reminded me of myself
the summer I failed
at selling *Time* and *Life* in New Jersey.
Even though I was a boy
I could feel someone else's voice
crawl out of my mouth,
spoiling every word,
like this cowed, polite kid in his tie
and badge that said *Greg*,
saying *Ma'am* to my wife, calling
me *Sir*, retailing the air with such piety
I had to find anything out the window.
Maybe the rain. It was gray
and as honestly wet as ever. Something
we both could believe.

Buying a Baseball

As I turned over in my palm
that glossy little planet
I was going to hand my son
I was wondering how
it could still cost the same
as when I was his age.
Around came the brand:
Rawlings. Made in Haiti.
Like those poor city kids
I'd heard have no idea
that milk came from a cow,
I'd never known before
where baseballs come from.
They were always there
in the stores in bins, stitched
tight as uncracked books,
each with its tiny trademark,
Made in Hell.
We'd test the tough seams
along both fingers' links
to get a thrill of power
remembering how to fake
a staggering grounder out
so it would leap to the mitt
at our convenience,
how that black magic squeezed
in the core would make it
spark off the bat
with a high, nasty *crack*
you could mistake for no
other sound in the world.

The History of the Wedge

In the brisk, pleasant voice of a surgeon
introducing his choice operation
the Air Force assured us how strictly
professional it is. *Armament,*
radius, objective: each word neutral
as a steel tool rinsed and drawn clean
from the Latin: a scalpel, a sterilized needle.
And we watched the latest knife:
five General Dynamics F-16s
like a five-card hand on the prowl
curve out over downtown Topeka and cut,
break east with a spurt, a sharp
black smudge and they're off on a new
vector, they are carving together,
that whole hand is rolling over
like one moving card revolving itself
to flash all five spades at once,
chased by the ragged mass of their roar,
the heavy furniture they trundle behind them
being hauled, torn over every rough floor
in the sky, rolling over roofs, ripping
and mending as the sixth svelte blade
clicks into formation, completing
that steadily traveling phalanx;
and there in the hazy autumn sky
we see this oldest formation of power,
abstract force focused in one ghostly
capital letter: Δ. The idea cruises
above us this afternoon, meeting
no resistance at all, circling
as if looking for victims. Nothing up there
to rape, but it can't stop moving,
it's coming back low, flat over the field

to shock it for kicks, the whole
history of the wedge is bursting
straight up the sky, trailing white crêpe-
paper streamers in one, grand, Fourth-of-July
finale, fanfare proclaiming its victory,
Force flaunting itself, flexing
its engines, crowing, deafening us
with its form of laughter
as it lets its whole tool hang out
unsheathed, vertically, over 10,000 feet,
shaking it, shoving it in our faces.

Roller Coaster

This roller coaster was condemned
in 1925. You remember that, how the shingly
underpinnings creak as the cars go clacking
over them above. But you get in anyway.
The guy that takes your tickets, like some
cheap abortionist's assistant, wipes his
hands on his ass, he doesn't care much
if you live or die. So you hang onto this
paint-chipped bar the way you'd bite
the pink eraser the quack doctor gave
you to keep from swallowing your tongue
as he starts to put you under, cranks
the seat up for the operation, up over
the midway in the night air seeping up
from Lake Hopatcong's seedy plumbing
up to the top, and suddenly it's
all true what they said: you were crazy
to come here. Hang on, bite, this operation's
on, you want to faint, you can't, he's taking out
this dirty pocket knife, this spoon, but
the anesthetic isn't working, you're going
to hemorrhage, the wind is rising in your ears,
ripping tears out, you've got to close your
eyes because you're going over the edge, he's
crazy, he's made a mistake, slipped, wham, the
chair's out of kilter, this is an emergency,
everything's coming apart in tatters, screams
fragments blowing past your ears, this guy is
crazy, he keeps on working, gnashing you around
but you've come out of it, you can remember
everything, the whole abortion, it's over,
your death's been pulled right out of your insides
like your breath, only you can get your breath
back again, you've come through.

"The Swing," by Honoré Fragonard

From this painting alone . . . one could have
predicted the entire French Revolution.
GERHARDT WEIS

Her pink chubby fingers trusting
the rope, one slipper flying
off one toy foot, a toy

herself, a girl is sailing through
the silly leaves. She hasn't heard
of the guillotine, she is plummeting,

rising into and out
of the pitfalls of pleasure,
her petticoats like a parasol blooming

over her Baron de Saint Julien
fainting in the bushes with desire
as she leaves him again to go high

into a leafy canopy that seems
to be connected to nothing—
How can it hang on any longer?

But she isn't thinking,
she's breathless, in a flutter,
a swoon as when, shopping, the mind

stops—We think, *This can be mine*—
and we give ourselves away just
as easily as this ignorant girl

secure on her plump velvet cushion
starting back down through the silly leaves
while the rope groans and holds,

now owning, now thoroughly
owned by the rush of the foliage,
by gravity.

River Time

Day after day we fell deeper
in love with gravity. Mornings
we could hardly wait to catch up
with the water. In tandem, making
aluminum shout over gravel, shush
up in the sand, I and my taciturn
friend from Minnesota would drive
our canoe down the bank at the river,
steady the boat for Tom's small son,
scramble in ourselves and then surrender.
"River time" we called it for a couple
of days, until we forgot the old time,
river time became absolute time,
the current our clock. We had struck
some common, rock-bottom pace.
We were drifting in step
with each floating leaf, with every
unblinking blister of foam
under the channel's silent spell,
no need to paddle
except to adjust to the ticking
current, trowel a slow whirlpool, a furl
filling up in the ripples we trailed,
correcting our timing to keep
in perfect stride with the law.

A dozen canoes, one canoe to a bend,
moving with the caravans of morning fog.
By noon everyone would be stoned
on pot and the hundreds of pounds
of beer we had brought.
The architect and his wife, all
the assistant professors, the various

students, even my friend in the stern
would be rendered inert,
complacent, unwilling to speak.
Whatever it was we might need
we would let the river decide.
We'd unbuttoned ourselves from our words,
we'd jettisoned the ballast
of the usual week, left all that
upstream on the bank. It made us
pleased with ourselves, day
after day, simply to register
the faithful way those banks continued
unfolding themselves and tree followed tree
through the warm, intermittent rain.
The rain meddled in everything.
It riveted the tarnished water, shooting
plump bolts through and through it,
spot-welding reflections of the sky.
The rain hopped all over your tarp
and in the hot swarm of your hair.
It was on your tongue, in your joints,
in the steam of your breath,
until you forgot to shoo off
the drops that alit, forgot
the wet yoke sticking tight to your back,
the hot swamps you lugged around
in both boots, forgot even the mush
squeezing foam between your toes.

Long before our last night on the river
we were wet beyond hope,
we could get no wetter. That night
someone's flashlight beam nicked
a flat rock with a necklace
curled on it—soft, precious—
a copperhead blocking the path.
In a hutch of clear plastic
anchored by rocks, we skinned
and steamed together. Outside, a bonfire

shooting twice as high as a man
gave its fierce work to an armload
of stones, coaxing them into embers.
We took turns steering to the tent
between tongs each red-hot rock
and scattered water on it,
making steam snarl, blinding
ourselves with blast upon blast.
Naked, whooping, we'd charge
at the river, then crawl back
in the blur of that stifling incubator
where we were babies again,
the language was skin,
you could forget even your name.
Of the girl who stole with me later
back to my tent I remember only
that she was wet wherever I parted her,
alluvial, how the graceful curved way
her hair fell seemed like a word
I had learned once—anonymous,
familiar. She was all words at once.
And I remember how, halfway
toward dawn, the cries of two
whippoorwills kept opening
and closing like twin arteries
while we answered each other.

Next morning, our last, the river
was iron, frying, leaping
in the light rain as people numbly
traded partners. I carried
my pack to the girl's canoe
and we took the current's smooth
old hand, let it take our hand,
our boat rhymed with the river,
and the drizzle lifted, the complexion
of the water cleared,
and we could see in the interior
the dark, slow slippage of bass.

Oars shipped, we watched a moccasin
give us the slip, scribble away
deep in that gray-green psalm.
And far out through the brush
and the mist's restlessness
a bobwhite swiped its whetstone.
We just let the boat drift,
pleased with the lull of inertia,
foreseeing no end, ready
for only what could be more water,
knowing that around the coming bend
across another misty clearing
the profile of the trees would be
unbroken, curving into the next
bend where another old tree
would be succumbing, tempted
to drink, its crooked reach
combed by the water, waking
the current under the cut-bank
before the water would widen
and we'd stall
in an even purer silence,
dim canyons of boulders, of twilight
deep in the green requiem below
easing silently under our bow,
the river adagio.

That afternoon, reluctant, we beheld
through gray, scarcely seeping air
stumps of a broken bridge
and down both banks a dump,
a great population of junked cars—
bodies which, once pushed, went churning
headfirst and, catching
on roots, had flipped on their backs
with the rest of the rusty scree—
a scorched city lost under the trees—
until the next bend gathered us
in, a crowd of people came slowly

around, walking on the rocks
where two trucks were parked
and a road—a shock of sky in the trees—
petered into the floodplain stones
and at the shallows stopped.
And two men, two fat retarded twins
in bib-overalls, two comical men,
humpty-dumpties with rotted mouths
were circling my Minnesota friend,
spitting words, gesticulating at him,
arguing he better move his goddamn
hippie van because this floodplain
here belonged to *them*, while Tom,
from the cab, glared down with a stiff
slightly puzzled stare, white-knuckled
in the face. And the look the architect
slipped me meant something dirty
he knew about, it meant *Move off.*
We walked our canoe across the ford,
shoved it up on mud. The rain
returned, through the rain
we watched one brother squat
behind Tom's camper to jot the plate.
Tom's truck wallowed, bucking in reverse
like a dog digging, spewing back rocks.
But the fat guy expected it. He lurched
the gap to his pick-up's cab,
and the long .22 automatic he pulled
discharged its six dried-twig snaps
at the back where Tom's boy bounced
as the rear of the fleeing camper
leapt over the crest and out of sight.

In fistfights the hate-scent can be so strong
it gets the tightening circle half incensed.
But anger, in a shot, goes so abstract
at first you can't even recognize it.
Just this detached small-kindling spark.
Could it be some practical joke

over which both brothers on the opposite bank
now chortled and whooped like Laurel and Hardy,
they were slapping their knees, congratulating
each other with whops on the back? *What time*
was it? All I knew was how wet and cold
and pathetic we looked, searching
for footholds in the mud, slipping,
digging in our heels again and heaving
our canoes up the bank—
how sick of this desolate river and the rain.
At last the road like a room in the woods.
Token of a hug was brusque enough good-bye
to the girl, who wanted to get away
as much as I did. And I talked
with the architect of what we'd seen,
our words—the words we needed—seeping
slowly back like heat into our extremities.
Then the small chagrin of comfort—
dry socks like Christmas presents,
the reassuring idle of a car—
our words now flooding back luxuriously,
words for that godforsaken place
and how to get out of it.
Later, with time enough to bathe,
the words for our excuses, the redundancies,
the first, sweet, foreshadowing
of shame.

Lust

You would have had to measure
that fair countenance of hers a hundred
times before you would suspect,
Susan was, when this was happening,
so beautiful. The finest murmur,
the slightest rumor passing in her face
you would have sworn implied a pure
intelligence, sworn that when
she looked amused at what you said
it was because her calm eyes
had read between the lines.
Only over time would you have seen
what I, too late, began to notice,
that she was always amused, her smile
was not authentic, there was
something covert about it,
it was askew, a thin moon
that stayed up far too long.
It was almost a smirk, a politeness
that mocked being polite
like her words, always a little too
sweet. Her answers, when, too late, I learned
to hear, would give you your own words
back, yet with the wrong taste.
But I was young and dumb,
her blond hair was proverbial,
and the body has its own rhetoric—
she was proof of that cruel joke.
So on this cold, windless afternoon
in the mountains when I hiked
over the Douglas firs' blue shadows
up the County Road to the mailboxes
by her house, knowing it was not

to fetch the mail, and opened
the side door at her muffled *Come in*,
stamping snow on the kitchen floor
and heard water plumping
from the hall bathroom where she called *I'm
here, come in*, I checked my watch and,
dumb as a man, calculated
how long the house would be secure—
this snug, strict little house so nicely
dusted and picked up, the winter
sunlight lost in the corners, discarded—
two hours until, upstairs, Leslie
would wake up.

The body, when it doesn't have
to explain itself, can be so
eloquent. An act of perfect
timing alone—a fake, a linked series
of strides to the hoop, the dunk—
looks exactly like intellect.
The move was *brilliant*, we say,
as if it were something we
had thought. Or think
of the beautiful stations of lust
linked, one after the other.
They form the perfect replica
of love—love, which is intelligent.
No matter how shrewdly each body
uses the other, you would swear
that both partners were true,
that they could trust each other.
You would swear, I think, to almost
anything, forgetting
the way an athlete hurt
on the field might be mistaken
for being, at that moment, sincere,
that the aftermath could be
as randomly littered with wreckage
as Susan's living room was

two Aprils later when, hailed
from the mailbox to be offered hashish
I looked the place over.
The divorce was soon to come through.
Plump Leslie sat dazed in a corner
while Susan and people I didn't
know, like a ring of campers
on the rug, warmed themselves
around the ashtray.
The house smelled all wrong,
but I lingered there simply to look
at Susan, imagining the earnest
almost clumsy way she had loved
to make our teeth bump, had licked
my back as that pink bath
slowly, all afternoon, sank
from lukewarm to cool around us.
I lingered just to look at her.
To look.

Some events, when held to the light,
you could pull like a sock inside
out. The day I accepted in a faint rain
Susan's ride up the mountain
in her old Dodge wagon with the shimmy,
Leslie, cherubic, her white German hair
cut in bangs, sitting in the back
with two other children,
it was simply to look at Susan
who, her stale smile a wisp of a moon,
with a ghastly pleasantry took every curve
up the canyon too fast.
She is insane. It was as if
I had owned the evidence all along
but hadn't known the right word,
that word which maybe always arrives
oblique like the oncoming
car which now did, as Susan,
stuck in her smile, not

slowing, spun the wheel
as if to turn into our side road,
and we came to rest, a stalled
windmill, intact in the other lane.
Then she turned the key and,
ignoring the children's slight
confusion, started the pull
up the wet dirt road, asking me
finally, as if somehow baffled, why
I seemed so nervous.
Do you know . . . how lucky . . .
I bumbled an answer, it was too
obvious. She just smirked to herself.
And when, on foot at last, I was
set free in the gray silence,
I must have been halfway down
the twin ruts to my cabin
when it struck me: she had tried
to kill us. I looked back, then.
Her car still hadn't moved.
It idled in the mist where she watched,
her want making me able to want,
want, even as I turned away.

Water Poem

Insurance breaks into poetry over water,
water's fickleness, its ignorance
of treaties—water knows no borders.
Against "flood, surface water, waves, tidal
water, overflow of a body of water
whether or not driven by wind, water
below the surface of the ground
including water which exerts pressure on
or seeps through a building," it will not
gamble, we're on our own. Working alone
caulking a skylight is a private matter.
One's solitude makes its single shadow
on the roof, both shoulders braced
against the sky in all its casual
magnanimity. The sky: today light enough
to carry on your back, an accidental blue.
Filling my steep driveway's ruts with stones,
how acute the foolishness I've felt.
The idea that one man could plot against
the weather; yet gamely I shoveled stones
into my wheelbarrow's rusty basin, let each
lapful of the rock I strained to steer
downhill pull me after it, jouncing on one
chubby tire to the gulley where I lopped
it down. When the next cloudburst
whitened the air, and the brown back
of the water arched, scuttling that hillside,
I knew those stones would be the only hands
I had to rake the brown rout for any dirt.
And after the storm, when the water
has found its subtle route back through the roof
and you have to read the script
which the torrent wrote around the stone—

paths much too exotic to predict—
as you stand there admiring such a waste
of work, what a loneliness that is:
You're every farmer, every engineer who lost
again, humming to himself the same flat
tune that all men learn as their insurance
breaks into poetry over water.

Casino

Under this oppressive slippery sky
of mirrors, where the promise of cash
is a fragrance, voluptuous,
you could forget the ways of the gods.
One pull on a handle, *bells! lights!* the world
could go all to pieces, be turning
itself inside out as if in love
with you. A slot machine spits
me a coin. I'm unmoved by gifts.
Luck, you can see, was never anything
less obvious than a lady slipping
her slightly fat shoulders from her robe
as she picks some victim out
to throw herself at.
And winning, though it's the perversion
hardest to resist,
may be more dangerous than losing.
A man thirty years married once told me
how most of one wonderfully mild,
wronged Tuesday morning, after drying
the breakfast dishes, he lounged upstairs
in his marital bed,
committing deliberate adultery
with a family friend,
how the pale light of her body,
filling the room, contradicted
the worn shag rug, the famous old crack
in the bedroom ceiling.
The perversity of it awed him—
his shockingly clear sense of detail,
that this beautiful head, eyes half
closed, her hair slicked hard
around her temples,

could replace his wife's bruised face,
as we'd say, *in the flesh*, could be this
literal. He could no more stop
than could any of these broken people
release the handles that keep pulling
them, though they know as well as we do
that the next jackpot will drive them crazy,
how luck and adultery
are only two of the many low religions,
each waving its claim to make a word flesh,
and the gods remain abstract
as money, as love, as they ever were.

Rereading Old Love Letters

It's like deciding to taste the milk
to see if it's still good,
afraid that it isn't, afraid that it is.
Every envelope you're about to part
causes another abrupt shift
in the weather under your shirt.
There's such momentum left,
it carries you straight toward the same edge
where you first let the word *love*
slip and dropped a foot.
Some things can't be unsaid.
After every sigh has drained into the woodwork,
here all the words will be
as wet as they ever were,
still in the same beautiful script
dancing as blithely as it always did,
the unpremeditated code of what we call
"the heart." Never. Forever. Each word spun
like a new coin and still spinning,
the same brave lovers' jokes:
If only, when they were apart,
they could keep each other's tongues in bottles
as hors d'oeuvres, preserved like trout.
And their special secrets,
how even in that drab high room
what she called this "religious" glow
could somehow soften all of the edges
when once again they would build and fan
under walls of plaster their fierce low fire,
how between the surges they were so quiet
they were like an old couple reading
something impossible
by the warm low lamplight of each other's

faces. But silent, content
to let that interval go unhooked by a word,
remembering the years they had eaten desire,
only to grind it to words.
And now here those words are, every one
its own perfect rebuke.
To read now without belief would be
sacrilegious, as cruel an act
as violating the skin of a moving trout,
hooked, still wet and
leaping, leaping all over the boat.
You open the envelope
where you know all the sweet words were—
to get at these words, the words
you must eat.

2

Ramanujan

As my grandfather said, when he gave up pursuit of The Territory and learned to read: Maybe the secret personality, the essence, of this country resides not in clichés about American violence, American self-reliance, or the American frontier but rather in the domain of the purely aesthetic, in the dialect of the land itself—in the moods of its weather, in the half-attended chatter of a ball game on the car radio, in the shape of a thunderhead in the afternoon heat, in the edge of a season. To illuminate this essence, instead of resorting to analysis and generalization, you would attempt, by selective description, to clarify your life, bringing its essential elements up into subtle relief.
WILLIAM H. FINN, from *The Diaries*

"Early Sunday Morning," by Edward Hopper

Way off to the right out of the picture,
just coming over the horizon, is the center
of action. Armies are mustered there.
That's where the brass bands are playing
and all the news is about to be made. News.
It swarms, spawning in the chilly sky
until the blue above the rooftops quivers
with it. But little is left of the hubbub
by the time it settles on this deserted street
except a rumor of that ultimatum, a hint
of breeze that steals along the brick
storefronts, a whisper of gossip in the gauze
curtains of the second-floor windows where
most of us are still asleep, unaware
of the revolution headed this way, the news
a faint echo off the peeling window frames,
a thrill in the glass ball on the barber-pole,
a warmth on the squat hydrant's iron hide.
Every nook and cranny of the block is in suspense.
The news is alighting softly, a golden silt
on the gaunt brick. Nothing important has happened
here yet. But every outcrop on the block
is starting to pay attention.
One by one the windows are noticing it.
A few remain black, but not for long.
Nothing can resist.
It is aimed right up the middle of the street,
toppling long thin shadows before it,
deafening the eastern walls of the buildings,
drumming on the barber-pole, lining up
the identical shadows of every cornice
and making those shadows obey.

It is assailing the shop windows, is about
to invade the darkened stores;
it's poised to leap through the glass
and over counters, to lay hands on
the unmanned cash registers, to claim
the floor, to occupy the farthest corners;
its victory glints off the hydrant's helmet
in this silent block that could be anywhere.

What to Do with Time on Your Hands

After breakfast, see
how business is
in the clouds for awhile
and listen
to your body working.
On the south wall
take your shadow
by surprise, rehearse
the high leg-kick,
your fastball: a whiplash
for a strike. Grab
some old snow. Wedge it
and graze the outside
corner of a tree.
Whop one up the middle.
Call strike two.
The hour before lunch
spend imagining
making love with Sue,
a conversation all of
eloquent gestures, long
silences, intricate wet
sounds. Listen
to the ponderosa bark
creak, give in the warm
breeze, and think
how slowly a tree works,
how you hate school.
After lunch, study
the sky-map some more,
the day's geography.
In the northwest corner
it's still morning.

"Snap the Whip," by Winslow Homer

It's late May,
the field, the ridges elbowing each other
back into this brilliant day
a flagrant green as monochromatic
as pain.
It's probably noon.
The children's shadows are pieces of light
clothing they've shucked underfoot.
The boys have linked hands to form
a chain and are running as hard
as they can
to see who will be slung off.
One is already falling
head first, his arms out to catch
the earth that's about to catch
him. This picture makes me think
of time
the way a prison can
for a moment make me stop taking for granted
my freedom.
Inside it
the children are running so hard
they think of nothing
but the solid pain in their lungs
and the sweet resistance in their arms.
Out here we serve
time for the rest of our lives.
We go free.

Saturday Morning

You're trying to keep
your dreams going by
carefully scraping their warm
ashes together.
Through the wall comes this *clunk*,
wincing of crib-springs,
bare feet smooch the floor.
A squeal, then giggling.
The toy school-bell rings.

Cars whir down the ramp
of the toy garage.
The musical clock starts
to tock. The children
are already open and doing
business, they've started
the city up again, hammering,
hurling blocks, turning
the cranks, utterly
loving their jobs.

Lines Written from Central Kansas

This pale spring afternoon, as I
scrape at my porch, alone, a little
portable radio on, gagging with static,
grasping at wisps of music, voices, fading
innings of the Kansas City game, I know
how the world ignores us,
that most of us were never anything
but lost down here under this commercial
weather of radio waves, faint
fleeing contrails of jets—left out
of some heaven, consigned
to this sort of life
sentence that started for me back
in New Jersey, the fifties, July nights
of steam clogged with wisteria.
And I think of that scene in *Picnic*
where Bill Holden hits the high board
hard with a whoop, flipping his tan back
out of the air
into an algae-hemmed pond.
Every high-school girl turns her wet
seal's head. And of Kim Novak. The black
craven rims of her eyes. Those eyes
wide open. Abject. Summer nights, stroked
by the loud fan, she hears the Rock Island
diesel horn shove its hoarse headline
forward, *Here!* a season of sound.
Madge, like a beautiful weed
waiting like the rest of us, ready
to go soft in advance. Ready for anything
else than could ever be where she is.
But waiting anyway, in whatever warm evening,
only to be found.

Cutting Loose on an August Night

Roll the windows all
the way down and keep it
floored until you can hear the doors
between the corn-rows bursting
open with the August hay
and the full force of the packed earth
being unpacked and shredded
up with speed as the center line
pours tracer bullets
at the bug-spattered windshield
and the night's rush outshouts
static on the radio
where New York trails Cincinnati
and Oklahoma City's
cutting in to say high
tomorrow in the mid to upper
90s, low, and a full slate
of night action out there
like dusty fairgrounds
fierce under arc light roars
no runs, no hits, no errors, one
man left, and the entire north
winces, takes the snap-
shot of a cloud
formed like a horse's head,
and you are fixed firmly
in the cool pressure of the night,
the glare of the Philadelphia
and Boston games as sure
as constellations,

you're weightless
in the thick of speed, going
nowhere in all directions
at once, nothing but the pennant
race at stake.

I Lie Awake on Top of the Sheets

It's the crickets. It's
the minor entry which
each cricket makes
filing its name,
trying to make it stick
in the humidity.
It's what my mother
used to call "peepers"
patiently cranking
out their lists,
each teeny mouth an open
wound repeating the same
signal, *This is an*
emergency. It's the sum
of all the raw nerves
mustered out there
in the night's sweet pits,
writing the encyclopedia.
It's too much. It's
the nights I used to lie
after a shower
when the trees were wet
broccoli dripping in
the dark, the stars
were safely set
in their places,
the air defused,
but the night was still rife
with prodigious tales,
the east would leap and
leap again with light
revealing the vivid
outlines of a continent

where crime after silent
crime was being committed
as the retreating forces
like distant AM stations
went on flashing the late
news excitedly, broadcasting
over the horizon.

Full Moon, Rising

So low it used to seem almost
perverse, like the risen dome of some dead
city, the full moon, rising, might have been
an omen—a public event
looming so great all roads would lead to it.
Whichever way I'd turn
on the small playground
I could not avoid it,
I'd find myself walking toward the moon,
though it is long since, now, that I have learned
what the full moon portends—
nothing, except that when you notice it
you're apt to be alone.
A name, someone you still love, comes to mind.
You remember, just then, that the earth is turning,
and feel, for a moment, certain
that as you notice it
you are the only one.

Scraping the House

Two rungs from the top, where you can see
what no one else could see, there are no more
handles on the world, I have to lean
against the warm cliff-face of my house,
cheek to cheek with wood, and, butting
the chisel's butt end crosswise with one palm,
drive it, balking, under the lapped siding
to strip more cracked paint off, baring
more evidence.
                                        Below, I hear my children
laughing. A screen door slams. They don't suspect
I'm here. They don't care. The beautiful lie
of this October afternoon maintains
its poise, steadfast as those brilliant aisles
the sun is laying down over the grass
in layers. The end of weather. You almost
believe it. That somehow the damage is not
serious. And you will always wonder why
when no one says you must, you keep coming back
here anyway, obediently, all by yourself,
to this ladder on the northwest side
for your appointment, and go up quietly.

Tinkering

It's a smug knowledge, to feel
your crescent wrench congruent
with a nut, the nut go *yes*.
That certainty—we remember it
like something we've deserved.
I understand exactly why
psychiatrists prescribe such
things for those recovering from
the grief of a great passion. Sweet
leverage—there is a logic
you can grab and trust, weigh
right in your arms, help it
gang up against a bolt
to make your bicycle, let's say,
recite its ABCs; you can know
how at least a few facts hold
themselves together, and it's sweet
the way the bike reciprocates
when you coast, to accept
the gift such easy distance is,
your front tire adrift,
tinkering along, moving
for nothing, explaining gravity.

On a Mild October Evening

Rope smarts the asphalt,
Adele in the middle,
the Lamberts' girls turning
the warm slack pages
of this evening
which like the full moon
has called the whole neighborhood
out. Bicycles swoop
Dr. Bark, who can't throw
anymore like a man, lofts
a flare pass for a short
gain. Lightfooted, I lope
along, keeping my daughter's
bike from tipping too
far as I dodge,
stutter-step cracks
like a man skipping rope,
until my daughter wades
forward, deeper, out
of my reach,
and the sidewalk is in shade,
stranded on the bottom
of the evening.
The sun's parting shots
miss, high wild,
nicking the treetops,
the sky still an ebullience
of birds, tilting
with the luck of the light,
testing their balance, taking
the late, brilliant
corners,
and the street is ambushed

by something greater
than shadow, it is time
to call the children in,
and the moon has unsnagged
itself from the elm,
rides free so early,
when I want to keep skipping rope
and learn to ride a bicycle
all over again,
to be called home by somebody else
as I used to be
just as the dusk started
to turn cold.

Jim

When Uncle Jim came back from World War II
there was something wrong with him.
He hid behind sunglasses, and he sulked.
He was sultry as an afternoon with thunderheads.
We hardly saw him. He stayed in the sour
little room upstairs my parents kept for him.
An entire summer Jim moped there, shades
drawn, sprawled in the yellowing rubble
of his sheets, studying the ceiling
and working on his schemes while the hot
little radio beside him gagged with static
and Mel Allen's play-by-play of Yankee games.
The only time he peered out, it was to pad
downstairs to the kitchen for a beer.

My father's simian-faced and spare,
a scientist; he is severe.
His mouth is as definite as a trap door.
He never knew how to do anything but work.
He still knows the third conjugation of Latin
verbs by heart. It scared him almost over
into hatred to have his younger brother
lying up there day after day not doing anything.
He didn't show it. He stumped about his business,
bought the beer. At night he'd read.
He rarely talked to me.

Jim knew the things I had, at nine,
to know: the nestle of an M-1's butt,
how hard it kicked, the ground speed
of the Lockheed F-80 Shooting Star,
how in artillery you had to yawn
so your ears wouldn't be hurt
when a howitzer went off. He taught me

how to talk cocky to take care of a bully,
DiMaggio's average, and all the junk
that Eddie Lopat threw.

Each week my father drove Jim to Madison
where Jim leapt up on the two-car
Lackawanna train that carried him
sadly into Irvington to see his bookie,
Hoppie, and a V.A. psychiatrist.
Jim had this dream that he'd disappear
for years, swore when he drove back he'd tow
an extra golden Cadillac for Father.

His last summer with us, I remember Jim
outdoors, swimming vaguely like a drowning man
around in molten light, still implacable
behind his shades as he and Father
sweltered together, swinging at bedrock
for the swimming pool, swatting mosquitoes
between blows. Each evening Jim prodded
me and my new J. C. Higgins bike down
the driveway to where the road glimmered
like a brook, stagnant under the thick
banks of the bushes. In the green,
backed-up water of the twilight,
Jim taught me how to swim.

Gripping the bike seat's nape
at the bottom of my back, Jim held me up.
Together we treaded water toward Pardees' trees.
Jim jogged along beside me, then let go.
I'd flounder, fighting the sticky fists
of that tin Ferris wheel until the thing
out-wrestled me and pinned me down;
but just as I was about to drown on gravel
Jim's hand was there to stand the evening
up again and steady it.

Once, Jim let go. With one thrust I
surged. Somewhere ahead of me a great
dam burst, the whole, backed-up current

of the evening began flowing with delicious
little lapping sounds around me.
My bike was sweeping me away downstream.
I was alone and swimming in slow, steady
strokes, not sure quite where I was,
but Jim's hand wasn't there.
I couldn't even hear his feet.
I didn't care.

I could push the bushes past.
I could make the road roll under me in swells,
pump that road up into choppy waves
that seethed beneath my tires, beat
gently against the bottom of my seat.
I could make the woods beyond the bushes march,
the whole world gradually move in synchrony
before I let the bike spill out from under me,
crash like an armful of dishes.

When Jim moved to Irvington that fall
to make his fortune, he left his radio beside
the bed. My parents papered his old room
for me with bucking cowboys.
I sent him a letter with my drawing
of an M-1. I never got one back.
We never heard from Jim again.
It didn't matter to me much, not even then:
I'd learned from him all I had to know.

Recessional

Son I call him—
such a serious word
it sobers me to say it—
as if I'd dropped
into his arms a weight
he could not let go—
the whole, drab encyclopedia
of *conduct, duty*—
words so obsolete
simply to utter them
would make the afternoon
slow as Latin.
I do not know
myself why, though our fathers
have passed from this world,
I would want one,
why, still, at the graduation
recessional, when the armies
in the chapel organ roll
and the grand old chords
unfurl their scrolls
of dusty laws, I feel
that weight gather
like Rudyard Kipling, brow
thunderous,
and even though I don't
believe in it
I know the urge
to look up to that tall
weather, a coward,
and hear my own small voice
call *Father*.

The Scientist

Other fathers might cuss out a lawnmower
that wouldn't catch Or kick the car.
Mine would simply stop. A physicist, he'd stop
and think awhile, his breath wheezing
through his nose—hiss and hiss, mechanical
until, abruptly, a solution clicked.
Then, step by step, arranging parts
in the sequence they'd come loose,
he'd direct at our lawnmower a logic
even that sullen machine could not refute.
Then, just as systematically, refit
each wrench upon its peg-board silhouette,
re-index every drill bit, every nail—
this small, half-German intellectual
who, although he'd own no gun himself,
let me wear twin Lone Ranger cap pistols
on each hip. You couldn't tell
just what he thought of you. Had he hated
us, he wouldn't have shown it. When,
in that reasoning, mildly troubled tone
of his that meant he might
be disappointed in his son, he once explained,
In war, people hurt with tools,
I shuddered. You couldn't imagine what
he might invent. He was a patient man.

Fireworks

My son could spend a whole afternoon
breaking dead sticks across the backs
of trees, or winging flat stones as if to ask
the air again and again the same thing.
Watching him test the resistance of the world
like that, unable to quit until
somehow he might provoke it,
I remember how we used to touch
off loops of homemade black powder
with a match, leaping back as it turned
cobra on us, furious. We couldn't stop
taking such measurements.
When, lighting a fuse, I'd dare
some hazy Saturday to answer with a bang
big enough to sober us all up,
it didn't matter if that flash
flattened the air out for a square
mile with one blow, it didn't matter
how hard I dwelled on it.
No bang was loud enough.
We had to hear it again
to believe in it, hear it again
before the dank air sealed
and we were left with the thin
Prussian-blue wistful tang of smoke—
the afterscent of passion—
the sunlight irresolute on the gray garage—
left with the crickets, old traffic sounds,
those small, standing laws of averages,
nothing to shoot off except
this light, dry ammunition.

The Kite

This is what the clouds lean
against. The pressure
which makes their lazy edges
fume. This lightest
suggestion of resistance
teases me. Something
I pluck at. A pure curve
I would extract out of the boundless
afternoon. It booms now
out of the air, burgeoning
over the grass, the idea enormous,
airborne, slender wisp
of a suspended bridge
taller than the evening
yet unfinished. As if the outline
of god's forearm glinted
an instant, caught the light.
The hint of a vector. Vanished.
The stick buzzes and leaps
in my hands, and spidery knots
follow each other, twirling
and twinkling into the altitude
where resistance simplifies
the string, smoothing it out,
making the stick throb
in my palms, which welcome
what resists, what bends this
span, pure stroke after pure
stroke, defining the actual
edge of each rock and plotting
the curve which every shadow
will trace around its stone
until the wind sinks, my kite

sets, and all the possible
curves are broken at once and
crumple lightly down the sky
and the limp span will not
support the weight of another
word and the string lies
crippled on the grass.

Night: Driving the Blizzard

—NEAR WAYNE, NEBRASKA

No clear landmark, yet I recognize
this: the first faint outskirts of fear.
No change in terrain. Just the suspicion
that the white roadside has gotten
much bolder, is venturing farther out.
Now the first white gap
as the shoulders close in and shut. Abrupt
silence. A break in the tape. No
more information. Just white. I make it
across. But when the dry pavement
resumes, both edges parallel,
and the snow is the same as it had been,
dancing over the road from left to right,
white rhyming with white,
I no longer trust anything.
I know what all kids learn in school,
there is not a single rhyme in the snow,
and every fancy design I see,
each cornice like a fine-sanded mantelpiece
is phony, invented
by the same wind that sends
the flakes slinking over the road,
lets them go slack or makes them fall backwards
and now in one huge gust gives all
the cold careless silks of the air
a toss so that they roll ahead of me,
curling out into gauze lingerie, teasing
along the spine of the road, evolving
into wisps of cirrus, caresses, scarcely
whispered suggestions, phrases
already coming apart into spirits
whirling away as if my headlights
were chasing these shapes

and I've let myself be fascinated again,
I had almost forgotten what I should know,
it is what could keep a man sane,
how exactly this chaos, when not seen whole
but only in glimpses, mimics order
even as the wind combs the snow back
into parallel lines, not real lines
I tell myself, there are no lines in this,
knowing I don't see it all.

Tornado Symptoms

As you step outdoors you'll enter a hot barn
with a moist haystack inside.
The cardinals will dart like embers, *pierce*
pierce your nerves with their bent sabres.
You'll be intimate with traffic for miles around.
But if you look up where the twigs
all stiffly point, you'll see silent
pandemonium, ugly rumors,
vagrant clouds loitering at loose ends.
It's a schizophrenic air.

By supper the sky will be uprooted,
a garden hopelessly gone to seed.
Gray broccoli will float by disconnected
from the ground; fat sooty toadstools,
a species you've never seen before,
will sprout beside swollen fungi
and other gray growths, strange weeds trailing
their severed roots, flowers the color
of bad bruises just opening into blossom,
slowly moving areas of combustion.
Even cauliflower as it rolls past
will be misshapen
before the forest comes.

The Mercator Projection

On the Hammond Mercator Projection of the World
Greenland is green and still huge
as when I first beheld it as a child,
climbing over the last bleak ridge of the north
where high as Hudson's Bay and even higher
the solid ground begins to come apart
opening toward the colder gray horizon.
The pole's too terrible, too white
to think about, it's off the map.
                                        We know
it's wrong, we know that on a map this flat
you never see the true shape of Alaska.
Yet we construct the map by such refusals,
refusing not to hope that the flattest
picture of Alaska is the truest.
So I refuse. I'll have the world both ways:
the Mercator Projection to be accurate,
the true North Pole a place we'll never go.

Facing West

When the moon rose that winter
the mountains shone,
a dim white cliff. No depth—
just a white fact of the moonlight,
an immense encroachment of silence
across the stars. Alone
I would pace the west window that faced
the mountain. Up there, lost
in that white drift of valley, rock, and ice
lived a woman, was the single
part of the world I truly loved.
Against the night, how minute it looked.
A speck? Less than that: a point
hidden beyond the first pale range, and high
where it was palpably darker,
the stars so bitterly bright, direct on the ice,
the moment you shut your headlights off
a cold vacuum descended on the roof.
I'd face west, oriented toward one small room,
its stark interior a laboratory
where what we'd distilled was kept pure
and potent—all the weather
that moved through her beautiful face
as the sun would choose the different windows,
deepening, dividing the morning
into another human landscape.
If there's any place in this world
where you are welcome—
some part that is loyal, no matter how far
or how infinitesimally

small—that tiny, moist place
you keep on your own person,
you carry it with you. Facing that
direction, you face
all the places you live.

An Introduction to New Jersey

The Eskimo has fifty words for snow.
AN ANTHROPOLOGICAL TRUISM

Consider our gentler tundra,
say U.S. 3 West, near midnight,
the slow, spiralling climb
out of Lincoln Tunnel—
how as you rise the whole
midtown skyline rises with you
like a wall of lighted newsprint
while columns of headlights
floating queasily somehow hold
formation, though every driver's
drunk—how the viaduct
finally slings all lanes off
strict west toward Secaucus,
Newark, Delaware Water Gap,
side by side at seventy,
the Empire State a lighted target
fastened to your back while
all about you flakes of light
fly faster, the news grows thicker,
pages of it coming up behind
you, turning in the mirror—
how I still, by heart, remember
where certain lanes for no
apparent reason peter out.
There's help in Montclair,
I would say, handing my car keys
to the Eskimo, knowing
he wouldn't live five minutes
out there.

Kansas Fair

There can be no such thing as a "normal life" until every oppressor swine has ransomed with his blood the blood of this brave lad.
FROM AN I. R. A. FUNERAL EULOGY

Sorefooted, sunburnt, I escape
the hot pelt of the crowd for a little
shade, to watch from the sidelines
people trading places. A baby,
eyes bugging, bobs by in its knapsack.
An old couple, in pursuit
of something severe and private,
hesitate, then find their narrow
seam through the traffic.
And as I sit there, pulled
by the argument of every smell—
cigar smoke, french fries, suntan oil—
by the whole, complex, bittersweet
scent of the gathered human—I wonder
what it would take to convert
these farm hands with mustard streaks
on their beards, so they might believe
in history. A scuffle? An explosion?
The helicopter, a dark locust swarm
spinning down over the trees?
I do not believe in one history,
but that among us the believers
are the dangerous ones.
Their minds are elsewhere.
When they eye a crowd from the side
they are counting the bodies.
And that it's lucky to be in the shade,
to be so prodigally bored,
resting one's feet, certain that
all this afternoon and the next, nothing
important will happen.

Ramanujan

It was Mr. Littlewood (I believe) who
remarked that "every positive integer was one
of his [Ramanujan's] personal friends."
G. H. HARDY

This modest, mousy little boy from India
could reel off pi's digits to any
decimal place his classmates dared him to.
No mean feat. But for Ramanujan it
was a breeze. Pi was merely one of his
first cousins, in fact a favorite.
And his cousins were innumerable.
Each day when school let out he'd retire
to the silent playground where they waited,
a windless plot with neither sun nor moon.
A silent playground—it was a funny place,
part civilized and partly wilderness.
It had some cultivated sections, but
all the rows, like footprints in the snow,
simply petered out into a white
fastness that was neither far nor near.
There was no definite horizon there.

Without a word, Ramanujan would sit
down among his friends and question them.
Some were persnickety at first, but if
he scattered seed and sat still long
enough, they'd hop right up to him.
Like sparrows, they'd eat out of his hand.
And once a number had confessed, Ramanujan
was its intimate. Each face touched off
for him its sly Gestalt, it pulled the trigger
that the kindly puss of your old car pulls
as you pick it out among the traffic,
idling with its crotchety click-click;
it was the smell of home cooking.
When Hardy once casually remarked
that the integer one seven two nine

on a taxi seemed "quite dull," Ramanujan
quickened. Why no, it was the smallest sum
of two cubes expressible in just two ways.

When he died, his room was packed. The walls,
the clock, the close air bristled with his friends.
As he expired, softly they slipped off,
those countless cousins, all without a word,
without jostling a single speck of dust,
without leaving the slightest trace behind,
without touching anything, fled back
to haunt that playground where for thirty years
he'd shuffled out and sat. The rest of us,
still stuck here in the shambles, go right on
sneezing with the seasons and galumph around
grabbing the daffodils too hard, bruising
the fruit, ordering the weeds to state their names,
waiting for the scent after the thunderstorm,
the shot, the drenching accident, to be
the Ramanujans of experience.

This volume is the eleventh recipient
of the Juniper Prize
presented annually by the
University of Massachusetts Press
for a volume of original poetry.
The prize is named in honor of Robert Francis,
who has lived for many years at
Fort Juniper, Amherst, Massachusetts.